5- Minute the Pete Cat Stories

by James Dean

HARPER FESTIVAL
An Imprint of HarperCollinsPublishers

HarperFestival is an imprint of HarperCollins Publishers.

Pete the Cat: 5-Minute Pete the Cat Stories
Copyright © 2017 by James Dean
Pete the Cat is a registered trademark of Pete the Cat, LLC
All rights reserved. Manufactured in China.
No part of this book may be used or reproduced in any manner
whatsoever without written permission except in the case of brief
quotations embodied in critical articles and reviews. For information
address HarperCollins Children's Books, a division of HarperCollins
Publishers, 195 Broadway, New York, NY 10007.
www.harpercollinschildrens.com

ISBN 978-0-06-298230-8

Typography by Lori S Malkin
19   20   21   22   SCP   10   9   8   7   6   5   4   3   2   1

First Edition

Contents

Pete the Cat
and the
Bad Banana

Pete the Cat loves bananas. He loves bananas because they are sweet and tasty. Plus, bananas are easy to peel. Pete can use his paws to peel a banana all by himself. Good job, Pete!

Pete also loves bananas because they are healthy. They give him lots of energy to do fun things like run in races and play games. In the morning, Pete adds a banana to his cereal. Bananas taste great with Kitty Puffs and milk. Yum! Now Pete is ready for a great day.

But one day, Pete eats a bad banana.
The banana is gross. The banana is
mushy. The banana is yucky.
Pete's tummy hurts. "I will
not eat bananas again,"
Pete tells his mom.

Pete's mom tries to help. She bakes Pete's favorite: banana bread.

It is warm and fluffy, but Pete will not touch it. "What if it's yucky like the bad banana?" asks Pete.

Pete's mom keeps trying. She makes
Pete a banana cream pie. Pete will not eat
it. She makes Pete a big banana split.
"No thanks," Pete says.

Pete is still hungry for a snack. Pete tries a lemon. It is yellow like a banana. "Maybe it will taste good like a banana," says Pete. He tastes it. "Yuck!" says Pete. The lemon is sour.

Pete tries a pickle. It is long like a banana. Pete tastes it.

"Better," Pete says, "but not as good as a banana."

Pete tries an orange. Pete can peel it all
by himself like a banana. Pete takes a bite.
The orange is sweet, but it is too juicy.
It makes Pete's paws sticky.

Pete keeps trying to find a new favorite snack. Pete tries fish, rice, plums, hot dogs, watermelon, and his mom's nut bread.

Pete eats them all! He is not hungry for snacks anymore. Pete is very full!

One morning, Pete is getting ready for a big race. He is going to need lots of energy if he is going to win. He usually has a banana for breakfast before a big day. But not today!

Pete wonders what he should eat instead.

A pickle? No, Pete doesn't eat pickles for breakfast!

A hot dog? No, Pete just had a hot dog for dinner last night.

A lemon? No. That's just silly.

Pete sees his friend Greg the Monkey eating a banana. That's all Pete wants. Bananas are yummy and healthy. Bananas are the best!

Pete decides to give bananas another try.
"Do you have another banana?" Pete asks.
"Of course," says Greg the Monkey.

Pete is nervous to eat the banana. He peels it slowly and looks at it closely. It is not brown. It is not mushy. Pete takes a teeny, tiny bite. It is a yummy banana. It is the best banana ever!

Now Pete has lots of energy to run and run. Just as they approach the finish line, he runs just a little bit faster. Pete wins the race. Everyone cheers!

"Thanks for the banana," says Pete.

"Thanks for a great race," says Greg.

Bananas are Pete's favorite food
to eat again. He is absolutely bananas
for bananas!

Pete the Cat
Go, Pete, Go!

It's a beautiful day, and Pete the Cat has decided to take his bike for a ride. Nothing makes Pete happier than feeling the sun on his fur and the breeze on his face.

Vroom! Vroom!

Turtle drives up to Pete in a race car. "Wow," says Pete. "Cool race car."

"Thanks," says Turtle. "I just got it. I want to see what it can do. Who wants to have a race?"

"Not me," says Grumpy Toad. "My motorcycle has a flat tire."

"Not me," says Emma. "My car is too old and slow."

"Not me," says Callie. "My bus is a work of art. It's not meant for racing."

"I'll race you," says Pete, knowing how much Turtle likes to race.

"But your bike has no motor," says Turtle. "My race car is super quick. I'll win for sure."

"That's okay," says Pete. "I just want to try my best and have fun."

Everyone is excited for the big race.

"On your mark. Get set. Go!" Callie shouts.

Turtle steps on the gas pedal and—
vroom!—zooms away.

"Check this out!" shouts Turtle. He presses
a button and . . .

. . . fins appear!
Now Turtle's race car goes even faster.
Vrrroom! Vrrroom!
Pete waves good-bye and then pedals off.

Pete's bike doesn't have fins, but it does have a basket. He stops and takes out a tasty red apple.

Nothing is better than a tasty red apple on a beautiful day.

Turtle sees that Pete is WAY behind. He spies a diner up ahead. "Might as well grab a bite to eat," Turtle says as he pulls into a parking spot.

"Yum!" says Turtle, eating a grilled-cheese sandwich. He is in no rush. He is sure he will win the race.

"Dessert?" the waitress asks.

"Don't mind if I do," Turtle says.

While Turtle finishes his lunch, Pete continues pedaling. The sun is high and the breeze is blowing. It's a beautiful day for a race.

Pete sees Turtle leaving the diner. Pete waves hello, but Turtle doesn't wave back. Turtle just jumps in his car and peels off.

"I guess he didn't see me." Pete shrugs.

But Turtle did see Pete. He knows that Pete isn't going to give up easily. So Turtle presses a button and his tires inflate into mag wheels that let him swerve around the curves at top speed!

Vrrr-vrrr-vrrrooooom!

Turtle sees that he has a HUGE lead. He knows he's going to win.

He stops for a nice, cold glass of lemonade, and that's when he sees the hammock hanging between two trees. He's exhausted from racing so fast. He figures a quick nap will help him in the home stretch.

Pete pedals past and sees Turtle sleeping.
That's cool, Pete thinks as he rides by as
quietly as he can. "Turtle must really be tired.
I'm glad he's getting some rest."

Grumpy Toad finds Turtle fast asleep!

"Wake up, Turtle," says Grumpy Toad. "If you don't get back in the race, Pete is going to win."

"That's impossible," says Turtle, thinking it must be a joke.

But it's no joke!

Turtle presses a button and rocket boosters appear, making him go super-duper fast.

Vrrrrrooooooooooooom!

But by the time Turtle nears the finish line . . .

. . . Pete has already won the race!

"How did you do it?" Turtle asks.

"Slow and steady," says Pete. "Maybe next time instead of racing, we can ride together."

"Great idea," says Turtle.

Now that Pete has won the race, it's his turn to drink lemonade in the hammock.

"What a great race. What a great day," Pete says.

Pete the Cat
Sir Pete the Brave

Meet Sir Pete. He is the bravest and coolest knight in all of Cat Kingdom! He wears a suit of armor and a helmet. He even carries a sword!

All day long, Sir Pete does lots of knightly things. He rides a horse and climbs towers. At dinner, Sir Pete listens to Lady Callie play the harp. Lady Callie is awesome!

"Bravo!" Sir Pete yells at the end of each song. He claps louder than anyone.

One night, while Lady Callie plays beautifully, someone casts a spell.

And everyone falls asleep—even Sir Pete!

When everyone wakes up, Lady Callie is gone!
"Oh no!" says Sir Pete the Brave. "I know what
to do. I will find Lady Callie and save her!"
So off Sir Pete goes to save Lady Callie.

Yikes! Sir Pete falls into a giant hole! Who could have made such a huge hole?

The hole is a dragon's footprint!

"Follow the footprints!" Sir Pete says to his horse. The dragon must have taken Lady Callie.

The footprints stop! Where did the dragon go?
Sir Pete looks up . . .

. . . and sees the dragon flying across
the lake with Lady Callie and her harp!

Sir Pete can't fly. How will he get
across the lake? He gets an idea. He can
row! Across the lake he goes!

Sir Pete gets to the other side of the lake. He spots a dragon cave! The dragon and Lady Callie must be inside the cave. He has to go inside, but it is very dark.

Then he hears music. He must save Lady Callie.
He won't be scared. He is Sir Pete the Brave!

He follows the music. But it suddenly stops. He
finds a harp. But no Lady Callie. Where could she be?

Sir Pete will not give up. He sees a hill and
decides to climb it. From there, he can probably see
Lady Callie. At the top of the hill, he looks around
for his friend.

Then he hears a loud growl. Sir Pete is scared. The hill suddenly starts to move! What's happening? Oh no. This is not a hill. . . . Sir Pete is on the dragon's back! He did not find Lady Callie, but he found the dragon!

Sir Pete knows what to do! He slides down, down, down the dragon's back as quickly as possible. Hopefully the dragon does not eat Sir Pete.

The dragon feels something ticklish on his back and sees Pete! The dragon lets out a mighty roar. Sir Pete is in trouble. Then out of nowhere, he hears a familiar voice.

"Sir Pete!" says Lady Callie. "I will save you!"

"Save me?" says Sir Pete. "But I came to save you."

Sir Pete and Lady Callie start to argue about who is saving who. They stop fighting, though, when it starts to rain. But wait. There are no rain clouds inside a cave. Sir Pete and Lady Callie look up and see the dragon crying.

"What's wrong?" asks Lady Callie.

"I just wanted to sing along," the dragon sobs. "But people get scared when they see me, because I am so huge and have sharp teeth. I did not want to scare anybody."

Sir Pete and Lady Callie feel bad for making the dragon sad.

"I have an idea!" says Sir Pete. "Will you give us a ride?"

The dragon flies Sir Pete and Lady Callie home. Everyone is happy to see them. At first they are scared of the dragon.

"He's our friend," says Lady Callie. Everyone is no longer scared of the dragon. "You don't need a great voice to make music," says Sir Pete. "Just good friends!"

The dragon smiles! He can finally sing
along. The dragon joins the song. Three cheers
for Lady Callie and Sir Pete the Brave!

Pete the Cat
Rock On, Mom and Dad!

It's Monday morning, and Pete the Cat wakes up, only to realize he is already running late for school. His alarm didn't go off!

Oh no! This is definitely not how Pete wanted to start out the week. But Pete is not worried at all. He quickly gets dressed. He knows his parents are here for him.

When he gets downstairs, Dad has already prepared breakfast.

"Better not skip breakfast. It's the most important meal of the day," says Dad. Pete chows down on cereal.

Pete gets ready to leave the house.

"Aren't you missing something?" asks Mom. Pete almost forgot his backpack! Good thing Mom had it all ready for him. He rushes out to catch his bus. Just in time!

Pete is thankful to have his parents to help him this morning. Pete knows that Mom and Dad do so much for him.

After Pete gets home from school, Mom helps him practice baseball. Pete is getting better and better every day with her help.

Dad takes him to his guitar lessons every week so Pete can practice what he loves. Pete's favorite hobby is playing the guitar.

Every day, Mom and Dad do a hundred little things. And Pete realizes that he's never really said thank you.

Today Pete is going to surprise Mom and Dad with something totally awesome. Pete tries to think of the very best way to say thank you. He could make them dinner. Except he knows he would probably make a big mess in the kitchen. Mom and Dad would end up helping him clean the kitchen instead. Not a good idea.

He could pick them a bouquet of
flowers. Except he is not sure what
Mom and Dad's favorite flowers are.
Pete thinks harder.

He could clean the house. . . . Mom and Dad
would like that! But the last time he vacuumed,
he broke a vase and almost broke a lamp.

He could mow the lawn . . . as long as he remembers not to mow the garden this time.

Or he could change the oil in Dad's car. But he was not too sure how to do that.

That all seems nice, but it doesn't seem like enough.
Pete really wants to do something special that they'll
never, ever forget. He wants them to know how thankful
he is to have them around.

Pete asks his big brother, Bob, for some help. Bob is the smartest guy he knows. Bob will know what Pete should do.

"What can I do to tell Mom and Dad how much I love them?" Pete asks.

"It doesn't matter what you do," Bob says. "It's how you do it. So long as it's from the heart, Mom and Dad will totally dig it."

That gives Pete an idea. He knows exactly
what to do to show Mom and Dad how grateful
he is. There is one thing Pete can do better
than any other cat he knows. . . .

Rock out.

So Pete sits down and writes Mom and Dad a song. Soon he is ready to perform the song, and it goes a little something like this:

Mom and Dad, you are the best.
I love you more than all the rest—
Yeah I do.

I cannot count all the things you do.
I know it's all because of you—
Yes it is—
That I love music and I love art
And I love you with all my heart. Yes I do.

"Wow, that was awesome," says Dad.

"And very sweet. We were not expecting this at all," says Mom.

It is the best surprise ever!

Pete the Cat's Train Trip

Pete the Cat cannot wait to visit his grandma with his mom and his brother, Bob. They get to ride on a train!

"Make sure you don't lose your ticket," says Mom. She gives one ticket to Pete and one to Bob.

Pete looks up at the big board. "Our train
is leaving at ten o'clock," he says.

A train speeds by. "That's not our train.
That's a cargo train," Bob tells Pete.

It's finally ten o'clock and the train
arrives at the station. "All aboard!" calls
the conductor. Pete is so excited, he's the first
one on the train.

71

Pete's mom finds three seats together. "I can't wait to see Grandma," says Bob.

"I can't wait to explore the train!" says Pete.

The conductor comes to collect the tickets. Pete hands over his.

"I love trains," says Pete.

"Really? I can show you around if you like," says the conductor. Pete nods his head. The conductor gives Pete an engineer's hat.

"Great. Let me introduce you to the engineer," says the conductor.

Pete follows the conductor from car to car as the floor rumbles under his feet.

"Wow!" Pete says when they get to the caboose. "We're going over a bridge."

Pete sees his mom and Bob. They are
at the snack bar!

"I got this for you," says Bob.

Pete follows the conductor. He goes to the front of the train.

"Come in!" says the engineer.

"Wow!" Pete says. The engineer shows him the engine and how everything works.

The engineer shows Pete the train's brakes.
Look. There is a tunnel up ahead!

When they go through the tunnel everything
gets dark. Pete gets to honk the horn. *Toot! Toot!*
It's so much fun!

Once they are out of the tunnel, everything is light again! They're almost at Grandma's house. Pete better get back to Mom and Bob.

"Thanks for showing me around," Pete says. He learned so much about trains today.

"Anytime. Have fun with your grandma!" says the engineer.

Pete walks back to his seat, where Mom and Bob are. It is a much longer walk than he remembered. He stops and meets new friends along the way.

They live in different towns. They are getting off at different stops. What a groovy ride!

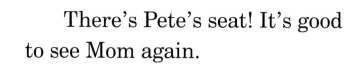

There's Pete's seat! It's good to see Mom again.

"We are getting off at the next stop," says Mom. Pete is happy he made it back to his seat in time. He can't wait to see Grandma.

Toot! Toot! Pete looks out the window and sees . . .

"Grandma!"

He waves at her from the window. Once the train doors open, Pete is the first one off the train.

He rushes over to give Grandma a big hug. It feels good.

"How was the ride over?" asks Grandma.

"It was groovy! I got a cool hat and met the engineer," says Pete.

Pete loves riding the train. He even drew
a picture of the train for Grandma. Grandma
loves it. What a special day!

Pete the Cat
Scuba-Cat

Pete the Cat is excited. He is in a boat on a beautiful day, and he's about to go scuba diving.

Pete puts on a mask and fins. He has a tank full of air so he can breathe underwater. He hopes to see lots of fish.

"If you are lucky, you might see a seahorse," says Captain Joe.

"A seahorse?" says Pete. "I can't wait! I've never seen one before."

"Their ridges look like a horse's mane," says Captain Joe.

"Groovy," says Pete.

Pete jumps into the water. He makes a big splash.
Down, down, down he goes. Up, up, up go the bubbles.
Pete looks for a seahorse. He sees a swordfish instead.
Pete swims out of its way so it can pass.

Pete waves to a stingray. It has a long, skinny tail.
That's not a seahorse, thinks Pete.

Pete feels a tickle on his leg.
Pete sees a school of fish. They all
look alike, except for a green one.

It puffs up. It is a blowfish!
It is not a seahorse.

Where could one be? Pete looks at the rocks. He sees something long and purple on the sand. What is that?

It is an octopus! It has eight legs. It is not a seahorse.

Pete feels another tickle as he swims. What could it be? Pete turns, but he doesn't see anything near him. He sees a cave! Is there a seahorse inside?

Pete sees a crab with claws. *A seahorse does not have claws*, Pete thinks. The cave gets darker as Pete swims forward. He is still looking for a seahorse, and he still feels a tickle on his leg!

Then Pete sees
an eel! It has ridges, but
they don't look like a
horse's mane. The eel is
too long to be a seahorse.

Pete keeps swimming farther into the dark cave.
Soon it is too dark to see! How will Pete get out?

Pete sees a jellyfish.
It glows in the dark. Now
Pete can swim his way out
of the cave.

He sees a striped angelfish. It is beautiful, but it is not a seahorse.

Pete swims out of the cave. *I wonder why it is still so dark,* thinks Pete. It's because Pete is in the shadow of a whale! Yikes!

Pete wishes he could jump on a seahorse and ride away!

Pete hops on a sea turtle instead. It takes him back to the boat. Sea turtles can swim fast.

I did not see a seahorse, thinks Pete. *Oh, well. I still had a great time. But what is tickling my tail?*

Pete turns and sees a seahorse! *What a great surprise!* he thinks.

Pete had felt the seahorse tickling his fur when he saw the swordfish, stingray, blowfish, octopus, crab, eel, jellyfish, angelfish, whale, and sea turtle.
You were with me the whole time, thinks Pete. *What a cool adventure!*

Pete the Cat Valentine's Day Is Cool

It was the day before Valentine's Day, and Pete was riding his skateboard home.

On the way, he saw his friend Callie. She was holding a big red heart that said "LOVE."

"Have you finished your Valentine's Day cards?" asked Callie.

"No. Valentine's Day is not cool," Pete said.

"Oh, Pete, Valentine's Day is my favorite holiday. It's a day to tell people how special they are to you," Callie insisted.

Pete skated on, but something in the back of his mind told him that Callie might be right.

By the time Pete got home, he had decided that
Callie was right about Valentine's Day. So he got out
his pencils, paper, crayons, and markers, and sat down
at the kitchen table.

First Pete started to work on a card for his friend
Larry. Pete made several cards with big red hearts, but
he was not happy with his work.

Pete wanted to make the perfect card for every cat in his class.

"I'll never get all these cards done in time," Pete told his mom.

Pete's mom smiled. "Just do your best," she said. "Just tell Larry why he is cool. There is something cool about every cat."

TO LARRY

HAPPY VALENTINE'S Day
FROM PETE

Pete got back to work. He thought hard about what was cool about Larry.

"Perfect," Pete said.

TO JOSH

TO ROB

TO TREY

After that, it didn't take Pete long to make cards for all the boys.

Then Pete made special cards for all the girls and wrote "Love, Pete" on each one. (And of course he made the biggest heart-shaped card for his mom!)

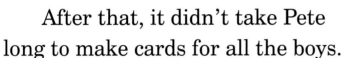

LOVE, PETE

FOR KIMBERLY

The next day, Pete and Callie waited for the bus together. "I decided you were right. Valentine's Day is cool."

"That's awesome," Callie said. "By the way, I am having a Valentine's Day party at my house after school, if you want to come."

The bus pulled up then, and Pete and Callie got on. Mr. Ted, the bus driver, smiled and said good morning, but as soon as they were in their seats, Pete put his head in his paws.

"What's wrong?" Callie asked.

"I forgot to make a card for Mr. Ted!" he cried.

Then Pete thought, *But I can make him an awesome card before we get to school*. Pete pulled out a piece of paper and colored pencils from his backpack. He began to draw.

"Happy Valentine's Day! Thanks for picking us up every day for school," Pete and Callie said as they handed Mr. Ted his valentine.

"Thank you," Mr. Ted told them. "You just made my day!"

"What about Mrs. Gold the crossing guard? We need to make her a valentine, too!" Pete practically shouted.

"Let's do it," Callie said. "Let's make valentines for everyone!"

Pete and Callie got super busy
making cards for everyone!

After school Pete went to Callie's party.
He rang the bell—and then he froze.

Callie opened the door only to find
her friend in a panic.

"What's wrong, Pete?"

"I forgot something very important," Pete admitted.

"What?" Callie asked.

"I just realized I forgot to make a card for you!" Pete said.

"That's okay, Pete. Cards are just a way of showing you care. Hanging out with you . . . that's way better than any card."

"This is the best Valentine's Day ever!"

Pete the Cat
Cavecat Pete

Cavecat Pete wakes up early. The sun is shining. The birds are singing.

Today is going to be a great day, Pete thinks. But Pete's bed starts to shake. His friend Vinny the Velociraptor is coming to visit.

"It's a perfect day for a picnic!" says Vinny, so excited that he jumps on Pete's bed.

"What a great idea," says Pete. "Who should we invite?"

"Everyone!" Vinny yells. Vinny does not know how to use his inside voice.

"Right on!" says Pete.

Pete love picnics! He jumps out of his bed to invite all his friends. It's Cavecat Times, so Pete has to walk everywhere.

First Pete finds his good friend Ethel the Apatosaurus!

To get her attention, Pete climbs all the way up to the top of the tallest tree.

"Would you like to come to a picnic?" Pete asks.

"I'd love to," says Ethel. "What can I bring?"

"How about a really big salad?" Pete suggests.

"What a great idea," says Ethel. "I love salad. I'm on it!"

Pete wanders along the river. He sees T. rex! T. rex plays guitar. T. rex is awesome! "Hey, T. rex," Pete yells, "want to come to a picnic?"

"Sweet," says T. rex. "Can I bring my guitar?"

"Definitely," says Pete. "We can jam!"

"Count me in," says T. rex. "Is it okay if I bring Al the Allosaurus? She's a whiz on the drums."

"The more the merrier," says Pete. "See you later!"

"Rock on!" they say.

Pete sees his friend Terri the Pterosaur in the sky.
"Hi, Pete!" she calls.

Pete invites Terri to the picnic, too. "Would you mind giving me a lift?" Pete asks.

"Sure," says Terri. "Climb aboard."

Pete sees the spiked tail of his main man Skip the Stegosaurus.

"How are you feeling today, Skip?" Pete asks. Skip has been sick with the sniffles.

"Better," says Skip. "Thanks for asking."

"You up for a picnic?"

"I think so," says Skip. "I'd hate to miss the fun."

It's almost time for the picnic! Cavecat Pete rushes through the forest. He doesn't want to be late. *What will all the dinosaurs talk about if I'm not there?* he thinks as he runs. Whoops! Pete trips over Trini the Triceratops.

"Are you okay?" asks Pete.

"Am I okay?" asks Trini. "I'm fine. I'm a dinosaur. Are you okay?"

"I'm okay, but I'm running a little—"

"We're playing hide-and-seek," Trini says before Pete can finish. "I think I hid a little too well."

"How long have you been hiding?" asks Pete.

"What day is it today?" asks Trini.

Pete thinks Trini has been playing hide-and-seek a little too long. "It's the day of our picnic!" says Pete. "All the dinosaurs are going to be there. Want to come?"

"Do I ever. Maybe somebody there will play hide-and-seek with me!" she says.

Trini and Pete head to the picnic together. Pete rides on Trini's forehead and holds on to her horns.

When they arrive at the picnic ground, everyone is there! Vinny and Ethel are setting up the picnic tables. T. rex and

Al are warming up to play some tunes. Terri and Trini are playing hide-and-seek. Even Skip seems to be enjoying himself!

"It doesn't get any better than this," says Pete.

T. rex comes over then.

"Hey, Pete," he asks, "is there anything else to eat? I'm a carnivore. I don't eat salad."

Trini comes over. "I can't play hide-and-seek with Terri," Trini says. "She's flying around peeking."

Skip comes over. "I don't feel so good," he says, and
he sneezes.

The dinosaurs all start to argue. It is very loud. The
picnic will be ruined if Pete doesn't do something. He
leans over to Al and says, "Can you give me a beat?" Pete
takes out his guitar, and he starts to sing.

Before long, everyone is having a great time.
"You know," T. rex tells Ethel, "I've never actually tried salad before."
"Try it," says Ethel. "I bet you'll like it."

T. rex tastes the salad. *Crunch, crunch, crunch.*
"Yum!" says T. rex. "This is delicious!"
Everyone grabs a plate and digs in.

After lunch is over, everyone wants to keep the picnic going a little bit longer. They decide to play hide-and-seek. Pete is happy that everyone is getting along. He feels lucky to have such great friends. Now he just has to find them.

After the game is over, they all cheer. Pete found all of the dinosaurs, even Trini.

"This was the best picnic ever," everyone says.

"It was the best picnic because you guys are the best friends ever," Pete says.

And no one can argue with that.

Pete the Cat at the Beach

It's a hot day! Pete the Cat climbs in the car with his mom and his brother, Bob. They have snacks, a surfboard, and a beach ball. They're heading to the beach!

Pete finds the perfect spot in the sand for their blanket.

"Let's go in the water," Bob says as soon as they've unpacked.

"Maybe later," says Pete. He watches as Bob swims out to catch the big waves.

Bob likes to surf. Pete likes to watch.

It doesn't take long for Pete to get hot sitting in the sun.

"I'm hot," says Pete.

"Why don't you join your brother in the water?" asks Mom.

"Maybe later," says Pete. He decides to make a sand castle instead. He is hot, but at least he's having fun. His mom helps him build the castle nice and tall. They're just about to put on the finishing touch when his mom says, "Here comes a big wave!" Pete jumps out of the way.

Pete's castle is washed away by the wave. *Bummer*, thinks Pete. He looks out at the water and watches Bob ride a big wave. "Wow!" says Pete. "That looks like fun."

"Come on, Pete," says Mom. "Let's take a walk."

There is lots to see on the beach. They find seashells, tide pools, and a crab.

"It buries itself in the sand to stay cool," says Mom.

Pete wishes he could be cool. He decides to get his feet wet. *Ah*, thinks Pete. *The water does feel pretty good on my hot feet.*

It's time for lunch. Bob swims in from
the ocean to join Pete and his mom. They eat
sandwiches and drink cool lemonade.

The sun is very strong. Pete is dry and hot, but
Bob is wet and cool. "It is so fun out there!" says Bob.
"I must have surfed one hundred waves!"

After lunch, Pete asks Bob to play catch with him.

"No thanks," says Bob. "I want to surf."

"I'll play ball with you," says Pete's mom. They toss the ball back and forth. They get hotter and hotter in the sun.

"Let's get our feet wet," says Mom.

"Okay," says Pete. "But just our feet." The water is cool. It feels good. Pete gets a little brave and goes deeper and deeper into the water.

Bob waves to Pete. "Swim out here so I can teach you how to surf!" Bob yells. Pete thinks about saying "maybe later," but the water feels so good. "Let's do it!" he says.

"Lie on the board," says Bob. Pete lies on the board.

"Paddle your paws in the water," says Bob. Pete paddles forward. He waits for a big wave.

A big wave comes Pete's way! "Stand up!" says Bob. Pete stands up, but he wobbles. It is hard to stand up on a surfboard!

Pete falls in the water. It was a little scary, but it did not hurt. He climbs back onto the surfboard. "Good job," Bob says.

"But I fell down," says Pete.

"That's okay," says Bob. "You'll stay on next time. Try again later."

But Pete doesn't want to wait. "Let's try again now," he says.

Pete lies down again. He paddles out and waits. "Here comes a big wave!" he shouts. *I know what to do*, Pete thinks. He stands up on the board. It's a little easier this time, and he rides the big wave!

"Wow!" says Bob. "Way cool, little brother!"

For the rest of the day, Pete and Bob share the surfboard. "It's okay to be afraid," says Bob.

"Yeah," agrees Pete. "But it is more fun to surf!"

Pete the Cat
Pete's Big Lunch

MAYO

BREAD

It is lunchtime,
and Pete is
ready to eat.

What should Pete eat? A sandwich might be nice.

Yes, Pete wants a sandwich. Pete opens the fridge.

He takes out a loaf of bread. He
finds a yummy fish. He adds tomato
and mayo. Pete looks at his sandwich.
Pretty good, he thinks. *But something
is missing.* He wants to add something
sweet. Pete knows what he needs! An
apple! Pete loves apples.

Pete's sandwich needs something else. Crackers! Every meal needs crackers. *They are crunchy and delicious,* Pete thinks. He uses a whole box. Pete looks at his sandwich again. It is still too small.

I wonder how much food I need to eat,
Pete thinks. *My stomach feels very empty.*

Pete adds a pickle, cheese, an egg, hot dogs, a banana, and a can of beans. Then to top it all off, Pete adds ice cream! He can't decide if he wants a scoop of chocolate, vanilla, or strawberry, so he balances all three on top of his sandwich.

Pete looks at his sandwich.
It is bigger than him! *How will
I ever eat that?* thinks Pete.
*Maybe I need a ladder or a
funnel or maybe something
to squish it down so I can take
a bite.*

I've got it! thinks Pete.
He takes out his phone and calls his friends.
He asks all of them to come over right away.

Everyone goes over to Pete's house.
I hope they're hungry, thinks Pete.

"Hey, Pete," they say. "Do you have any snacks?"
"I sure do!" he says. "Come on in."

Everyone takes a piece of the sandwich. There is plenty
to go around. They each get the part they like the best.

Now there is no more giant sandwich!

"Sharing is cool," says Pete.

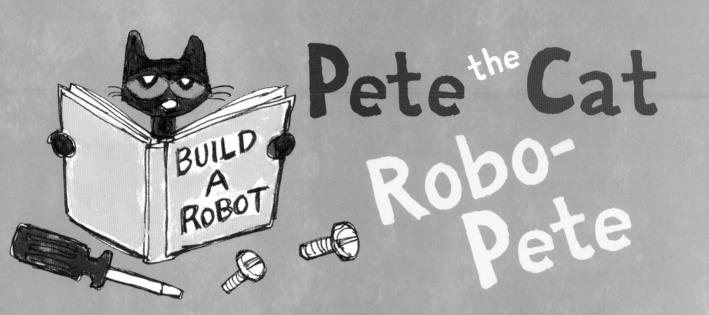

Pete the Cat
Robo-Pete

What a great, sunny morning! Pete can't wait to play baseball with his friends.

"Do you want to play catch?" Pete asks Larry.

"I can't," says Larry. "I'm going to the library."

"Do you want to play catch?" Pete asks Callie.

"I was about to go for a bike ride. Maybe later," says Callie.

"Do you want to play catch?" Pete asks John.

"I can't right now," says John. "I have to paint the fence."

All of Pete's friends are busy doing other things.

Pete wishes his friends would do what he wants to do. It's no fun playing catch all by himself. *If only I knew another me. . . .* Pete thinks. And just like that, Pete gets a great idea.

Pete builds a robot! He programs it to be just like him.

"Welcome to the world, Robo-Pete!" he says to the robot. "You're my new best friend. We'll do everything together. Want to play catch?"

"Great idea!" says Robo-Pete in his robotic voice.

Pete and Robo-Pete play catch.

"Wow!" says Pete, running after the ball. "You sure can throw far!"

Robo-Pete throws farther and farther until Pete needs to catch his breath.

"Time out!" says Pete. "I'm tired. Let's play something else."

"I want to play whatever you want to play," Robo-Pete says proudly.

"How about we play hide-and-seek?" says Pete.

"That will be fun," says Robo-Pete.

Pete finds the best hiding place ever! He's sure Robo-Pete will never find him.

"Ten, nine, eight, seven, six, five, four, three, two, one!" shouts Robo-Pete. "Ready or not, here I come!

"Gotcha!" shouts Robo-Pete, tagging Pete.

"How did you find me?" asks Pete.

"With my homing device," says Robo-Pete. "You gave it to me. I can find anyone, anywhere."

"Oh yeah," says Pete, a little disappointed. It's no fun playing hide-and-seek with someone who doesn't even have to try to find you. "Okay, enough hide-and-seek. Let's play some guitar."

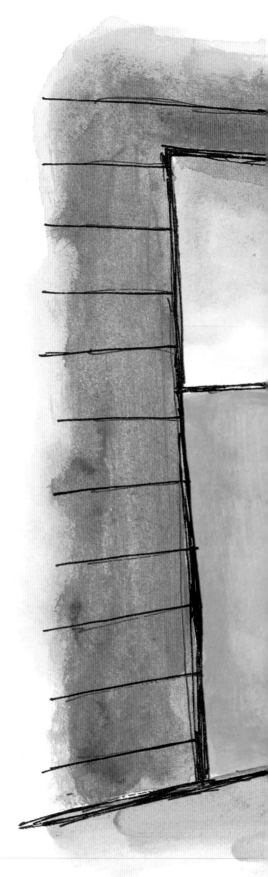

Pete teaches Robo-Pete how to play a song he made up. "You have to feel the music," Pete explains.

"Okay. The louder I play, the more I feel it!" he shouts over the noise.

Pete tries to stop Robo-Pete, but Robo-Pete can't hear him. Robo-Pete plays on and on.

Pete goes outside to ride his skateboard. Robo-Pete follows him.

"That looks like fun," says Robo-Pete as his feet transform into a motorized skateboard and a jetpack comes out of his back. "Thanks for the super speedy wheels!" he shouts as he takes off down the path.

"Wait!" calls Pete.

Pete chases after Robo-Pete. He has no idea where Robo-Pete is going until . . . *Crash!* Robo-Pete slams into the sandbox at the playground.

"Are you okay?" Pete asks his robot.

"I am a robot. I am indestructible!" says Robo-Pete. "What is this strange place?"

"It's a playground!" says Pete.

"My friends are here," says Pete. "Callie, Larry, John, this is Robo-Pete. I made him myself."

"Cool," says Larry.

"We are going to help John finish painting," says Callie. "And then we are going on a bike ride."

"I want to go on that thing!" interrupts Robo-Pete.
"Thing?" asks Pete as Robo-Pete zooms up the slide.
"Robo-Pete, I want to help my friends paint the fence."

"Paint the fence—that sounds great," Robo-Pete says. "I am programmed to paint faster than anyone."

Pete and his friends try to help, but Robo-Pete paints too fast.

So instead,
they ride bikes . . .

. . . and they read books, and after Robo-Pete is done
painting, they help him clean the brushes.

Pete realizes that it doesn't matter what they do.
Just being with his friends is what makes it fun!

Pete the Cat Construction Destruction

"Recess!" Pete shouts as the bell rings. But when Pete gets outside to play—oh no! The playground is a disaster. The swings are broken. The slide is rusty. And the sandbox is full of weeds. "How can we play out here?" asks Pete. "Somebody should clean this up." That gives Pete an idea.

Pete will build a new playground. He draws a plan for the new slides, tunnels, and swings.

"Wow!" says Principal Nancy. "Can you really build that?"

"Not by myself," says Pete. "I'm going to need some help."

"Whatever you need, Pete, it's yours."

PLANS for NEW PLAYGROUND

BY PETE the Cat

The next day, Pete arrives at the playground before school. The construction crew is already there. He gives them the go-ahead to tear down the old playground.

Creak! Crash! Down goes the slide.
Clink! Clank! Down go the swings.
Bang! Boom! Down goes the tower.
Honk! Honk! A truck arrives to
recycle the metal.

The new playground equipment arrives. It's
time to get to work. The cement mixer pours concrete.
The dump truck brings sand and dirt. The backhoe digs.
The whole team gets the job done. Building a playground
is hard work.

The new playground is cool, but it's not cool enough.
"What do you think?" Pete asks, holding up his latest
plans.

"It will be too hard to build," says one of the workers.

"And everything is almost finished," says another.
"But it will make this the best playground ever," Pete says.
"Then let's do it," the workers say.

Screwdrivers twist in screws.
Wrenches tighten the nuts. The workers
try to make everything perfect.

Hooray! The new playground is ready. Everyone is amazed, until . . .

Smash! Crunch! Thud!

"Oh no!" says Principal Nancy as the new playground crashes to the ground. "The pieces are all mixed up." Everyone is disappointed—except for Pete.

They rebuild the playground.
"It's not how we planned it!" Pete
shouts. "It's even better!"

This playground is filled with surprises
and places to explore. The school playground
is the most amazing playground ever.

Sometimes you've got to dare to dream big.